W9-CSL-564

In loving memory of
Dr. Earnest Corker,
who greatly influenced my
dream of becoming a
Veterinarian.

Dr. Terrence Ferguson

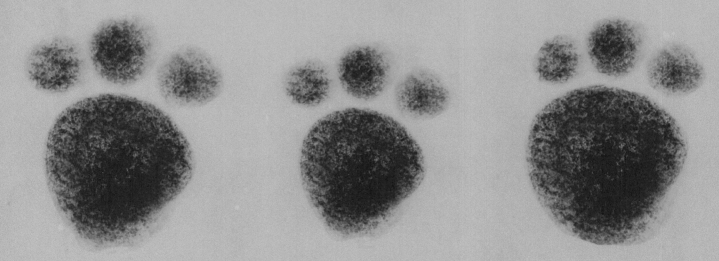

To the next generation of
dreamers:
Aamylah, Eli, Kaia, Ayva & AJ.

Annette Coward-Gomes

Most kids have no idea what they want to be when they grow up, but little Terry Thomas knew exactly what he wanted to be. He wanted to be an animal fixer.

It's important to have a goal in life.

Terry loved all kinds of animals, big ones, little ones, black and white ones, and brown and orange ones. He was always bringing home a stray animal he found in the neighborhood.

"Momma, Momma, I want to be a critter fixer," Terry yelled as he ran through the house.

"Whoa, heavens, slow down before you hurt someone," said Terry's mother as she grabbed him around his waist. "Do you mean, you want to be a *veterinarian*?"

"Huh?" Terry said as he raised his arms above his head.

"A veterinarian is someone who fixes animals, son," she said.

"Ohhhh, Momma, I get it. That's a very big word," Terry said.

"Yes, it is, and you can be anything you want to be. Just believe in yourself," said Terry's mother.

You can become whatever you want in life.

"Ok. But momma, but there's just one problem," Terry said as he lowered his big brown eyes. "I've never seen a critter fixer that looks like me," Terry said.

"Look at me son. What do you mean?" Terry's mom asked as she held his face.

"I've never seen a critter fixer with brown skin, so how can I be one?" Terry asked

"Terry, it doesn't matter what color your skin is, sweetheart," she said as she held Terry's face. "If you study and work really hard, you can be anything you want to be. Do you understand?" she asked.

"I do, Momma, I do," Terry said.

It doesn't matter if your skin is red, yellow, black or white, you can be whatever you want to be.

The next day, Terry found a little black dog curled up in a ball, and it was shaking.

"Hey, little guy, what's wrong with you? It's going to be ok."

Terry picked the dog up and carried him home to his mother.

It's important to take care of others.

"Momma, Momma, where are you?" Terry asked.

"What is it son, what's the matter?"

"I found this little guy in the park, he was shaking and crying!" Terry said.

"I know just the person to take him to. Let's take him to our local veterinarian, Dr. Talbot," said Terry's mother.

Dr. Talbot greeted Terry and his mom in the waiting room.

"Well, hey, everybody, let me take the little fella in the back and see if we can find out what's wrong with him. Looks like his leg is broken. It's going to be ok, little fella," said Dr. Talbot.

"Momma, Momma," whispered Terry with a wide smile on his face.

"What's the matter, Terry?" She asked.

"Dr. Talbot looks just like me, he has brown skin all over," Terry said.

"You see, I told you son, it doesn't matter what color you are, you can be anything you want to be," she answered.

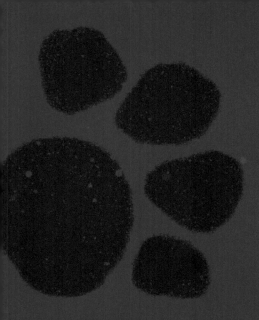

Dr. Talbot returned to the waiting room.

"Well, just as I thought, y'all. This little guy's leg is broken. He may have a little scar, but I stitched him right up. And in just a couple of months, he'll be back to his old self," said Dr. Talbot.

"Woo-hoo!" I told Mom you were a critter fixer," Terry said, laughing.

Dr. Talbot handed the dog to Terry.
"I sure am, now who's going to care for this little guy?" he asked.

Terry looked at his mom with tears in his eyes. "Please Mom, pretty please, can we keep him?" Terry asked.

"Terry, honey, animals require a lot of care and attention. You're going to have to help bathe, feed and walk him every day," she said.

"I can do it, Mom, I promise, I promise, scout's honor!" Terry said.

"All right, honey, we'll see how it goes. Let's get to the puppy store and get this little guy a few things."

"Woo-hoo!!!! You're coming home with us," Terry said as he hugged and kissed his new pet.

If you say you're going to do something, it's important to follow through.

Later on that night, Terry's mom walked in the room to say good night. Terry was under the covers, but he wasn't alone. Hiding under the covers was his new friend.

"Terry, the little guy is supposed to be in his own bed," she said.

"I know mom, I just want to keep him close," Terry said.

"Ok, but just for the night. And one more thing, you haven't named the little guy, what should we call him?"

"Lucky, we should call him Lucky, because I'm lucky to have him. One more thing Momma, I'm going to be a veterinarian so I can take care of animals just like Dr. Talbot," Terry said

"I believe you," said Terry's mom. "I want you to practice writing *veterinarian* every day because if you dream it, you can achieve it. Good night son, pleasant dreams," she said.

"Good night, Momma."

Dreams always come true.